MY BOOK

(not yours)

This book belongs to

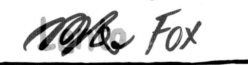

Fox

Ben Sanders

Kane Miller
A DIVISION OF EDC PUBLISHING

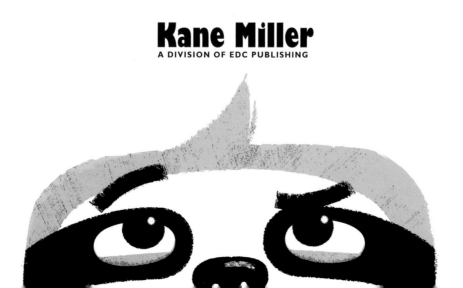

Dedicated to
SUCRE'S
STREET KIDS

First American Edition 2020
Kane Miller, A Division of EDC Publishing

© Ben Sanders 2019
The moral right of the author has been asserted.
First published in Australia in 2019 by Hachette Australia Pty Ltd.

Design by Ben Sanders
Typeset in Brush Up Copyright © 2013, Ricardo Marchin & Erica Jung
FONT-ON-A-STICK Copyright © 2002, Font Diner
Weeping Willow Copyright © 2018, David Kerkhoff

For information contact:
Kane Miller, A Division of EDC Publishing
P.O. Box 470663,
Tulsa, OK 74147-0663
www.kanemiller.com
www.usbornebooksandmore.com
www.edcpub.com

Library of Congress Control Number: 2019952267

Printed in China
ISBN: 978-1-68464-065-2
2 3 4 5 6 7 8 9 10

Hello, I'm Lento
and this is
MY BOOK.

nap.

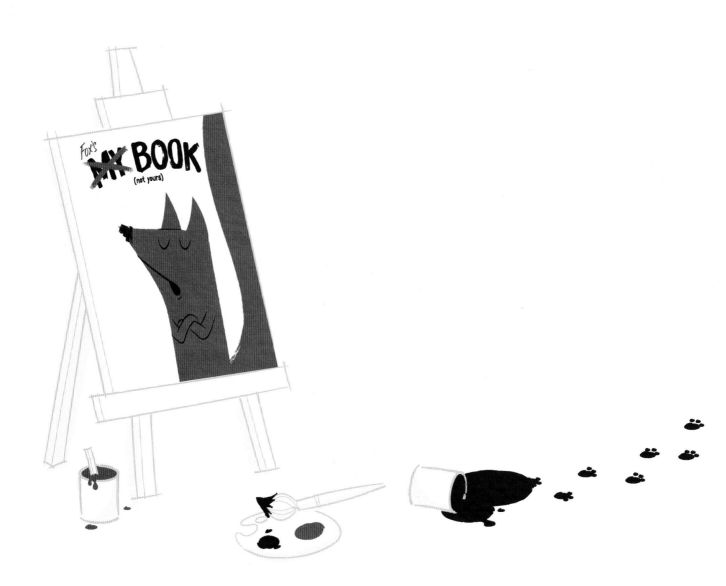

Wet
Paint